Tomorrow

A Personal Journal with Quotations

RUNNING PRESS
PHILADELPHIA · LONDON

There is nothing like a dream to create the future.

VICTOR HUGO (1802-1885)
FRENCH WRITER

Tomorrow is the most important thing in life. . . .
It's perfect when it arrives and it puts itself in our hands.
It hopes we've learned something from yesterday.

Today I begin life anew. Today I am born to a fresh, new, bright, glorious day.
This day has never been lived before and will never be lived again.

JACK AND CORNELIA ADDINGTON
20TH-CENTURY AMERICAN WRITERS

Forward, forward let us range,
Let the great world spin for ever down the ringing groves of change.

The present will always contribute to the building of the future.
FRANTZ FANON (1925-1961)
AMERICAN PSYCHIATRIST

... live your best and act your best and think your best today, for today
is the sure preparation for tomorrow and all the other tomorrows that follow.

Normal day, let me be aware of the treasure you are.
Let me not pass you by in quest of some rare and perfect tomorrow.

MARY JEAN IRION (B. 1922)
AMERICAN WRITER

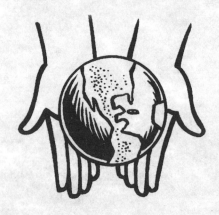

I am so absorbed in the wonder of earth and the life upon it
that I cannot think of heaven and the angels. I have enough for this life.

PEARL BUCK (1892-1973)
AMERICAN WRITER

Planning is bringing the future into the present
so that you can do something about it.

ALAN LAKEIN
20TH-CENTURY AMERICAN WRITER

The future is hidden even from the men who made it.

ANATOLE FRANCE (1844-1924)
FRENCH WRITER

Not until tomorrow will we see clearly enough
to appreciate the gifts of today.

RUTH SARGENT (B. 1920)
AMERICAN WRITER AND DANCER

Each birthday brings with it the potentiality of a new beginning,
new or renewed life, a symbolic new birth or rebirth, as well as marking
the passage, the end, or the symbolic death of the previous year.

JEAN SHINODA BOLEN (B. 1936)
AMERICAN WRITER AND PSYCHIATRIST

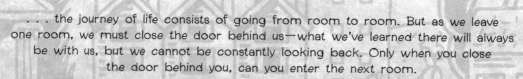

. . . the journey of life consists of going from room to room. But as we leave
one room, we must close the door behind us—what we've learned there will always
be with us, but we cannot be constantly looking back. Only when you close
the door behind you, can you enter the next room.

KIRK DOUGLAS (B. 1916)
AMERICAN ACTOR AND WRITER

When one door of happiness closes, another opens; but often we look so long
at the closed door that we do not see the one which has been open for us.
HELEN KELLER (1880-1968)
AMERICAN WRITER AND LECTURER

He who is outside his door already
has a hard part of his journey behind him.

The journey of a thousand miles begins with one step.

LAO-TZU (604-531 B.C.)
CHINESE PHILOSOPHER

He who would learn to fly one day must first learn to stand
and walk and run and climb and dance: one cannot fly into flying.

FRIEDRICH NIETZSCHE (1844-1900)
GERMAN PHILOSOPHER AND POET

We are all, it seems, saving ourselves for the Senior Prom. But many of us forget that somewhere along the way we must learn to dance.

ALAN HARRINGTON (B. 1919)
AMERICAN WRITER AND SOCIAL CRITIC

To accomplish our destiny it is not enough merely to guard prudently against road accidents. We must also cover before nightfall the distance assigned to each of us.

ALEXIS CARREL (1873-1944)
AMERICAN SURGEON

The fortunate circumstances of our lives are generally fo
at last, to be of our own producing.

OLIVER GOLDSMITH (1728-1774)
ENGLISH WRITER

It is the choices you make today that are creating . . . your future.

SHAD HELMSTETTER
20TH-CENTURY AMERICAN WRITER

We all stand on the edge of life, each moment comprising that edge.
Before us is only possibility. This means the future is open. . . .

ROLLO MAY (B. 1909)
AMERICAN PSYCHOANALYST

The future enters into us in order to transform itself
in us long before it happens.

RAINER MARIA RILKE (1875-1926)
GERMAN POET AND WRITER

We are tomorrow's past.

MARY WEBB (1881-1927)
ENGLISH WRITER

The years teach much which the days never know.

No single event can awaken within us a stranger totally unknown to us.
To live is to be slowly born.

ANTOINE DE SAINT EXUPÉRY (1900-1944)
FRENCH AVIATOR AND WRITER

How narrow our souls become when absorbed in any present good or ill!
It is only the thought of the future that makes them great.

GISELA MARIE AUGUSTA RICHTER (1882-1972)
AMERICAN WRITER AND ARCHAEOLOGIST

Forgiving is a way of reaching out from a bad past and heading out
to a more positive future.
SUZANNE SOMERS (B. 1946)
AMERICAN ACTRESS

We are not born all at once, but by bits. The body first, and the spirit later.

MARY ANTIN (1881-1949)
AMERICAN WRITER

. . . one does not merely grow and enlarge one's experience, but one loses earlier selves. We move forward into darkness, and the darkness closes behind.

JOHN UPDIKE (B. 1932)
AMERICAN WRITER

No matter where we go we take ourselves with us.
New vistas does not mean we lose our old ways.

GENE DAVIS
20TH-CENTURY AMERICAN EDITOR

We are not unlike a particularly hardy crustacean. . . . Each time it expands from within,
the confining shell must be sloughed off. It is left exposed and vulnerable until,
in time, a new covering grows to replace the old.

GAIL SHEEHY (B. 1937)
AMERICAN WRITER

Like it or not, we grow like onions grow, layer upon layer,
or like a tree ring upon ring, outward from its core.

FRED ROGERS (B. 1928)
AMERICAN TELEVISION PERSONALITY

Just as a snake sheds its skin, we must shed our past over and over again.

SIDDHĀRTHA GAUTAMA [THE BUDDA] (C. 563-483 B.C.)
PRINCE OF THE SĀKYAS AND FOUNDER OF BUDDHISM

When old words die out on the tongue, new melodies break from the heart; and where the old tracks are lost, new country is revealed with its wonders.

RABINDRANATH TAGORE (1861-1941)
HINDU POET

Growth is the only evidence of life.

JOHN HENRY NEWMAN (1801-1890)
ENGLISH CARDINAL

Far away there in the sunshine are my highest aspirations. I may not reach them, but I can look up and see their beauty, believe in them, and try to follow where they lead.

LOUISA MAY ALCOTT (1832-1888)
AMERICAN WRITER

. . . there are such things as second chances,
even if dreams go unanswered. . . .

KERI HULME (B. 1947)
NEW ZEALAND WRITER

When all else is lost, the future still remains.

All I can do is let this day come to me in peace.
All I can do is take the step before me now. . . .

HUGH PRATHER
20TH-CENTURY AMERICAN WRITER

Life appears to me too short to be spent in nursing animosity or registering wrong.

CHARLOTTE BRONTË (1816-1855)
ENGLISH WRITER

We must think new thoughts, we must love
as we have never even suspected we can love. . . .

HARLAN ELLISON (B. 1934)
AMERICAN WRITER

. . . to look back all the time is boring. Excitement lies in tomorrow.

NATALIA MAKAROVA (B. 1940)
RUSSIAN-BORN AMERICAN DANCER

Time does not become sacred to us until we have lived it,
until it has passed over us and taken with it a part of ourselves.

JOHN BURROUGHS (1837-1921)
AMERICAN WRITER AND NATURALIST

. . . what seems important today is probably not tomorrow. . . .

JANE HAMILTON (B. 1957)
AMERICAN WRITER

The future is no more uncertain than the present.

WALT WHITMAN (1819-1892)
AMERICAN POET

The future is called "perhaps," which is the only possible thing to call the future. And the important thing is not to allow that to scare you.

TENNESSEE WILLIAMS (1914-1983)
AMERICAN PLAYWRIGHT

Be not anxious about tomorrow. Do today's duty, fight today's temptations and do not weaken and distract yourself by looking forward to things you cannot see and could not understand if you saw them.

CHARLES KINGSLEY (1819-1875)
ENGLISH CLERIC

You don't have to be afraid of change.
You don't have to worry about what's been taken away.
Just look to see what's been added.

JACKIE GREER (B. 1909)
AMERICAN WRITER

In *every winter's* heart there is a quivering spring,
and behind the veil of each night there is a smiling dawn.

KAHLIL GIBRAN (1883-1931)
LEBANESE NOVELIST, ESSAYIST, AND POET

Such is the state of life that none are happy but by the anticipation of change.
The change itself is nothing; but when we have made it,
the next wish is to change again.

People themselves alter so much that there is something new
to be observed in them forever.

JANE AUSTEN (1775-1817)
ENGLISH WRITER

Old age is not an illness, it is a timeless ascent.
As power diminishes, we grow towards more light.

MAY SARTON (1912-1995)
AMERICAN POET

To grow older is a new venture in itself.

JOHANN WOLFGANG VON GOETHE (1749-1832)
GERMAN POET

We search for the meaning of life in the realities of our experiences,
in the realities of our dreams, our hopes, our memories.

The most important thing is not to stop questioning. Curiosity has its own reason for existing. One cannot help but be in awe when he contemplates the mysteries of eternity, of life, of the marvelous structure of reality. It is enough if one tries merely to comprehend a little of the mystery every day.

ALBERT EINSTEIN (1879-1955)
GERMAN-BORN AMERICAN PHYSICIST

Like a morning dream, life becomes more and more bright the longer we live,
and the reason for everything appears more clear.

JEAN PAUL RICHTER (1763-1825)
GERMAN WRITER

All our progress is unfolding like a vegetable bud. You have first an instinct, then an opinion, then a knowledge, as the plant has root, bud and fruit. Trust the instinct to the end, though you can render no reason.

RALPH WALDO EMERSON (1803-1882)
AMERICAN WRITER

We like to pretend it is hard to follow our heart's dreams. The truth is, it is difficult to avoid walking through the many doors that will open. Turn aside your dream and it will come back to you again.

JULIA CAMERON
20TH-CENTURY AMERICAN WRITER

Cherish your visions; cherish your ideals; cherish the music that stirs in your heart, the beauty that forms in your mind, the loveliness that drapes your purest thoughts, for out of them will grow all delightful conditions.

JAMES ALLEN (B. 1929)
AMERICAN WRITER

The truth is that there is never a really "right time." . . . there comes a time when one simply hopes for the best, pinches one's nose, and jumps into the abyss. If this were not so, we would not have needed to create the words heroine, hero, or courage.

CLARICE PINKOLA ESTÉS (B. 1943)
AMERICAN WRITER AND PSYCHOLOGIST

. . . we have not even to risk the adventure alone, for the heros of all time have gone before us. The labyrinth is thoroughly known. We have only to follow the hero path.

JOSEPH CAMPBELL (1904-1987)
AMERICAN WRITER

The greatest moments of growth
come at the times you feel totally helpless. . . .

Every tomorrow has two handles.
We can take hold of it with the handle of anxiety or the handle of faith.
ALEXANDER POPE (1688-1744)
ENGLISH POET

Never let the future disturb you. You will meet it, if you have to,
with the same weapons of reason which today arm you against the present.

MARCUS AURELIUS (121-180)
ROMAN EMPEROR

I have accepted fear as a part of life—specifically the fear of change . . .
I have gone ahead despite the pounding in the heart that says: turn back. . . .

ERICA JONG (B. 1942)
AMERICAN WRITER

People underestimate their capacity for change.
There is never a right time to do a difficult thing.
A leader's job is to help people have vision of their potential.

JOHN PORTER (B. 1931)
AMERICAN EDUCATOR

Someday change will be accepted as life itself.

SHIRLEY MACLAINE (B. 1934)
AMERICAN ACTRESS

Self-confidence is the first requisite to great undertakings.

SAMUEL JOHNSON (1709-1784)
ENGLISH WRITER AND CRITIC

To keep our faces toward change and behave like free spirits
in the presence of fate is strength undefeatable.

HELEN KELLER (1880-1968)
AMERICAN WRITER AND LECTURER

Life is change. Growth is optional. Choose wisely.

KAREN KAISER CLARK (B. 1938)
AMERICAN POLITICIAN AND ACTIVIST

The world is advancing; advance with it.

GIUSEPPE MAZZINI (1805–1872)
ITALIAN STATESMAN

Far off I hear the crowing of the cocks,
And through the opening door that time unlocks
Feel the fresh breathing of To-morrow creep.

HENRY WADSWORTH LONGFELLOW (1807-1882)
AMERICAN POET

Everybody, my friend, everybody lives for something better to come.

MAXIM GORKY (1868-1936)
AMERICAN WRITER AND HISTORIAN

I always had something to shoot for each year: to jump one inch further.

JACKIE JOYNER-KERSEE (B. 1962)
AMERICAN ATHLETE

The difference between the impossible and the possible
lies in a person's determination.

TOMMY LASORDA (B. 1927)
AMERICAN BASEBALL COACH AND MANAGER

. . . you have to make sacrifices and live creatively
to keep working at your dream.
ALEX HALEY (1921-1992)
AMERICAN WRITER

If you aspire to the highest place, it is no disgrace to stop at the second, or even the third . . .

MARCUS TULLIUS CICERO (106-43 B.C.)
ROMAN ORATOR, STATESMAN, AND PHILOSOPHER

He who gives his best today will be even better tomorrow.

WALLY AMOS
20TH-CENTURY AMERICAN WRITER

Every small, positive change we can make in ourselves
repays us in confidence in the future.

ALICE WALKER (B. 1944)
AMERICAN WRITER

I am not afraid of tomorrow, for I have seen yesterday and I love today.

WILLIAM ALLEN WHITE (1868-1944)
AMERICAN WRITER

I have always been delighted at the prospect of a new day, a fresh try, one more start, with perhaps a bit of magic waiting somewhere behind the morning.

J. B. PRIESTLEY (B. 1894)
ENGLISH WRITER

Throughout the centuries there were men who took first steps down new roads,
armed with nothing but their own vision.

AYN RAND (1905-1982)
RUSSIAN-BORN AMERICAN WRITER

Everyone has talent. What is rare is the courage to follow
the talent to the places where it leads.
ERICA JONG (B. 1942)
AMERICAN WRITER

Possibilities. . . . Tomorrow is about possibilities.

ANNE RIVERS SIDDONS (B. 1936)
AMERICAN WRITER

To me there is something thrilling and exalting in the thought
that we are drifting forward into a splendid mystery—into something
that no mortal eye has yet seen, no intelligence has yet declared.

EDWIN HUBBELL CHAPIN (1814-1880)
AMERICAN CLERIC AND WRITER

I compare human life to a large mansion of many apartments,
two of which I can only describe, the doors of the rest being as yet shut upon me.

JOHN KEATS (1795-1821)
ENGLISH POET

God made the world round so we would never be able to see too far down the road.

ISAK DINESEN (1885-1962)
DANISH WRITER

Tomorrow the world is not the same as today, though God listens with the same ear.

BERNARD MALAMUD (B. 1914)
AMERICAN WRITER

Life is a series of collisions with the future;
it is not a sum of what we have been but what we yearn to be.

JOSÉ ORTEGA Y GASSET (1883-1955)
SPANISH PHILOSOPHER, WRITER, AND EDUCATOR

. . . the future is not ominous but a promise; it surrounds the present like a halo.

JOHN DEWEY (1859-1952)
AMERICAN PHILOSOPHER, PSYCHOLOGIST, AND EDUCATOR